Colby's New Home

Written by Roxana Faith Sinex
Illustrated by Wendy Cowper-Thomas

BELLWOOD PRESS
Evanston, Illinois 60204

Bellwood Press, 1233 Central St., Evanston IL 60204-0605
Copyright © 2006 by the National Spiritual Assembly
of the Bahá'ís of the United States
All rights reserved. Published 2006
Printed in the United States of America on acid-free paper ∞

09 08 07 06   4 3 2 1

Library of Congress Cataloging-in-Publication Data

Sinex, Roxana Faith, 1952-
    Colby's new home / written by Roxana Faith Sinex ; illustrated by Wendy Cowper-Thomas.
        p.   cm.
    Summary: When Colby, an Asian American boy, moves to a new house and finds that the students at his school do not like to play with children of other races, he uses his kitten Fluffy to help him make friends. Includes a note to teachers and parents and three selections from Baha'i writings about unity in diversity.
    ISBN 0-87743-705-X (softcover : alk. paper)   [1. Racism—Fiction. 2. Prejudices—Fiction.   3. Asian Americans—Fiction.   4. Schools—Fiction.] I. Cowper-Thomas, Wendy, 1955- ill. II. Title.
PZ7.S61543Co2006
  [E]—dc22
                                                  2004018338

Design by Suni Hannan
Illustrations by Wendy Cowper-Thomas

For my father,
William Evans Price, Jr.
1924–2001

Big brown cardboard boxes filled the new house. Colby stared up at the towering stacks. They reminded him of his wooden blocks.

"Where are my blocks, Mommy?" Colby called out, hoping she could hear him.

"I haven't found them yet, Colby, but when you get home from your new school today, they should be unpacked and ready for you."

Daddy appeared from behind a huge box. He handed Colby his backpack. "It's time to go to school!

I'll show you where your new bus stop is."

Colby stopped to give his kitten a gentle hug on the way out the door. "Be good while I'm gone, Fluffy," Colby whispered into the kitten's tiny ear. "Stay out of Mommy's way, and don't run off and get lost!"

The bus stop was down at the end of Colby's new street. There was a big red stop sign on the corner. Colby saw some other kids waiting there. Feeling a little scared, he held Daddy's hand tightly. He could feel the children's eyes upon him. "Wait with me, Daddy," Colby said quietly.

Soon the big yellow school bus roared up to the bus stop.

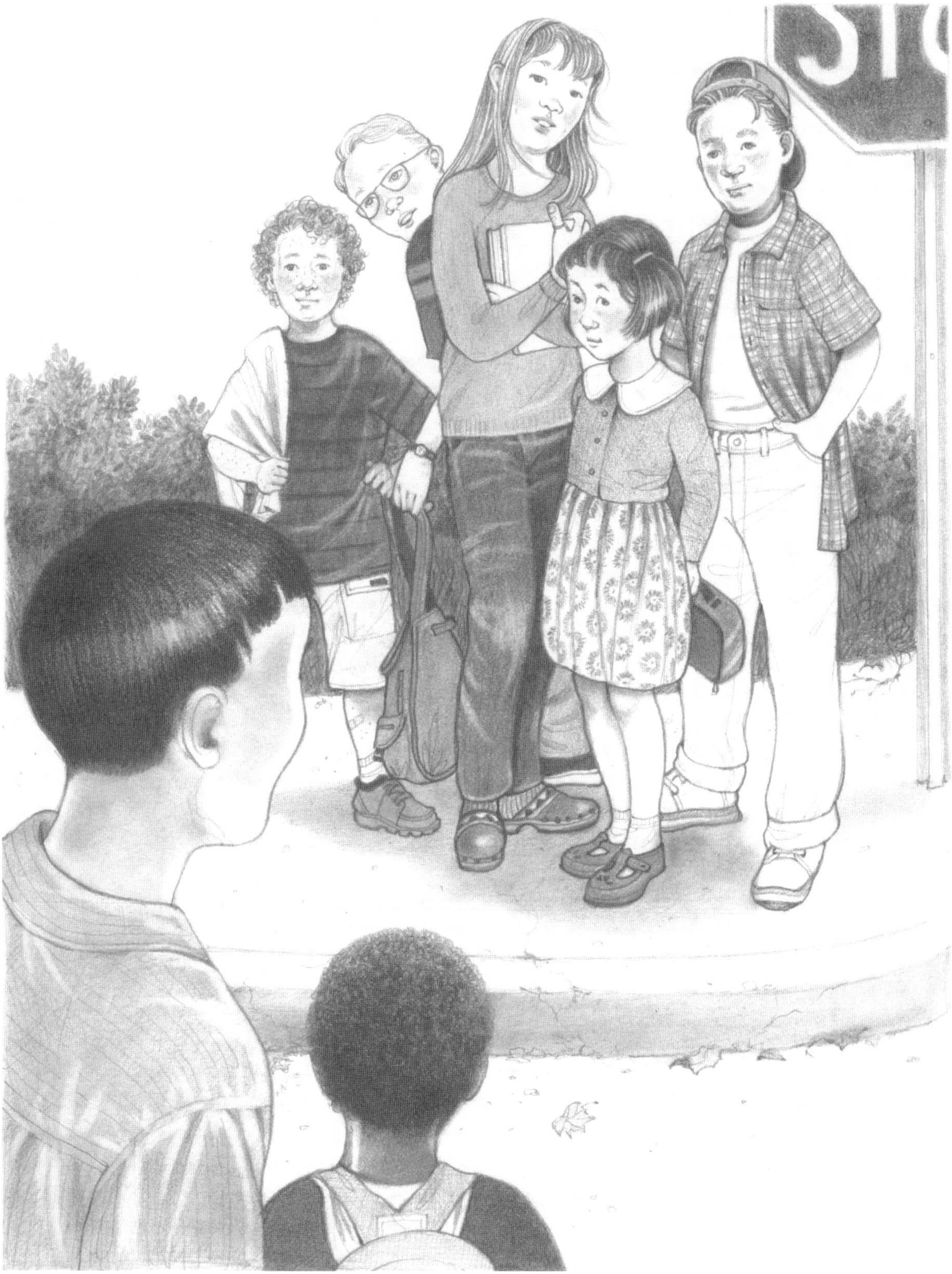

"Bye, Colby! Have a great day at your new school!" said Daddy, peeling Colby's small clammy hand out of his big warm one.

"Bye . . . !" Colby answered as he turned and climbed aboard with the other children.

The bus was noisy. Children were laughing and talking as it shuddered and jerked into the traffic. Colby sat quietly, listening to the others talk and play.

"Did you see his father?" Someone behind him said.

"He's got slanty eyes, like this," the voice said, giggling.

Then two high-pitched voices chanted the much-hated verse that Colby had been teased with before: "My mom's from Japan, my dad's from Siam, and I'm both!" This was followed by gales of laughter.

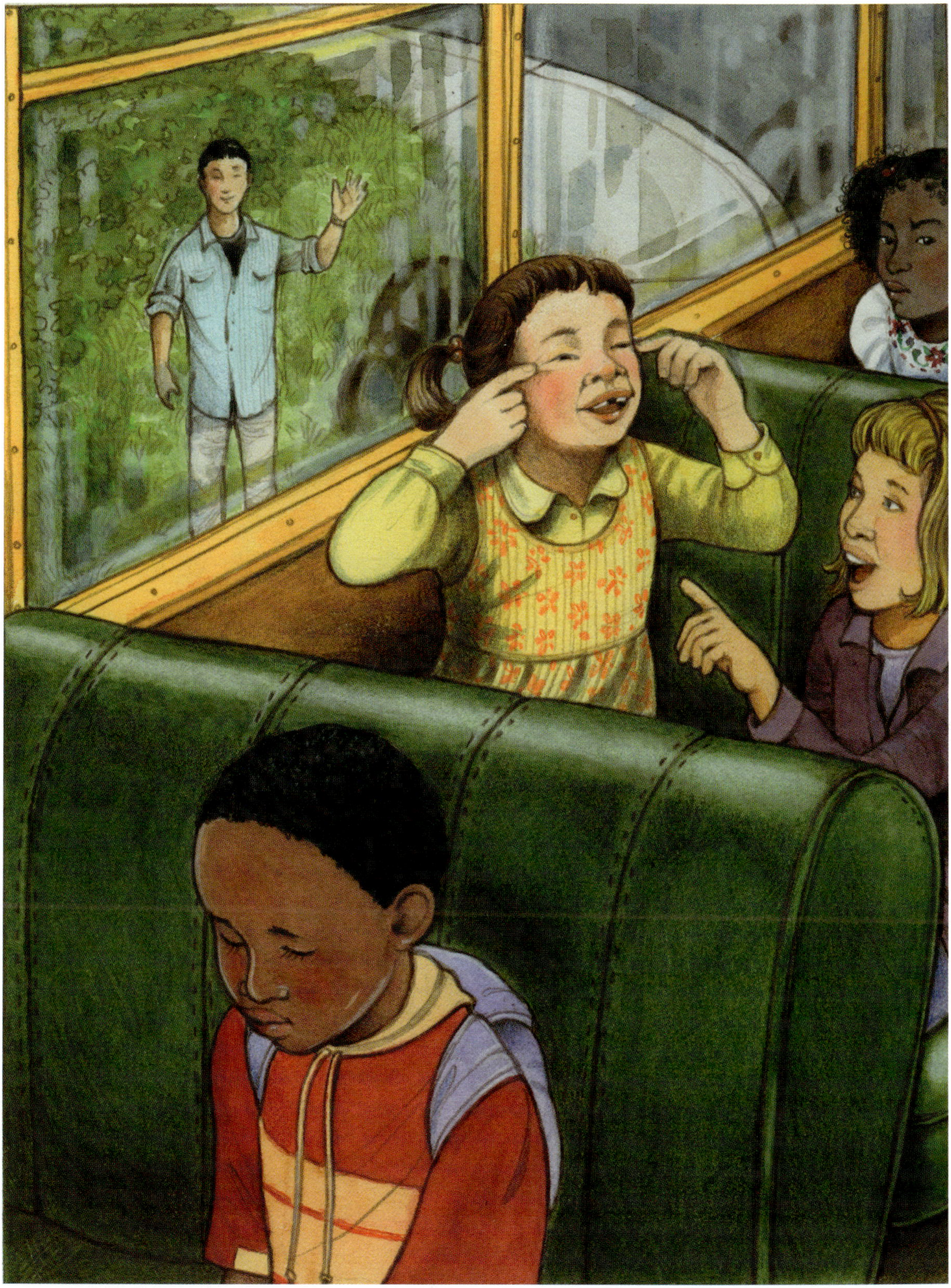

Colby imagined the two little girls behind him with their fingers stretching the corners of their eyes, one up and one down, in a ridiculous joke about Asian eyes. He felt like shrinking into a small corner where no one would see him. He wanted to go home.

When the bus arrived at school, there was a grownup who helped the children as they got off the bus. He showed Colby the way to the office, where someone was waiting for him, just as Mommy had said. The woman behind the big metal desk greeted him with a friendly smile, picked up some papers, and showed him to his new class. Colby was still feeling a little scared, but his teacher was very kind, and that made him feel better. He began to enjoy the morning as he learned where things were and when things happened.

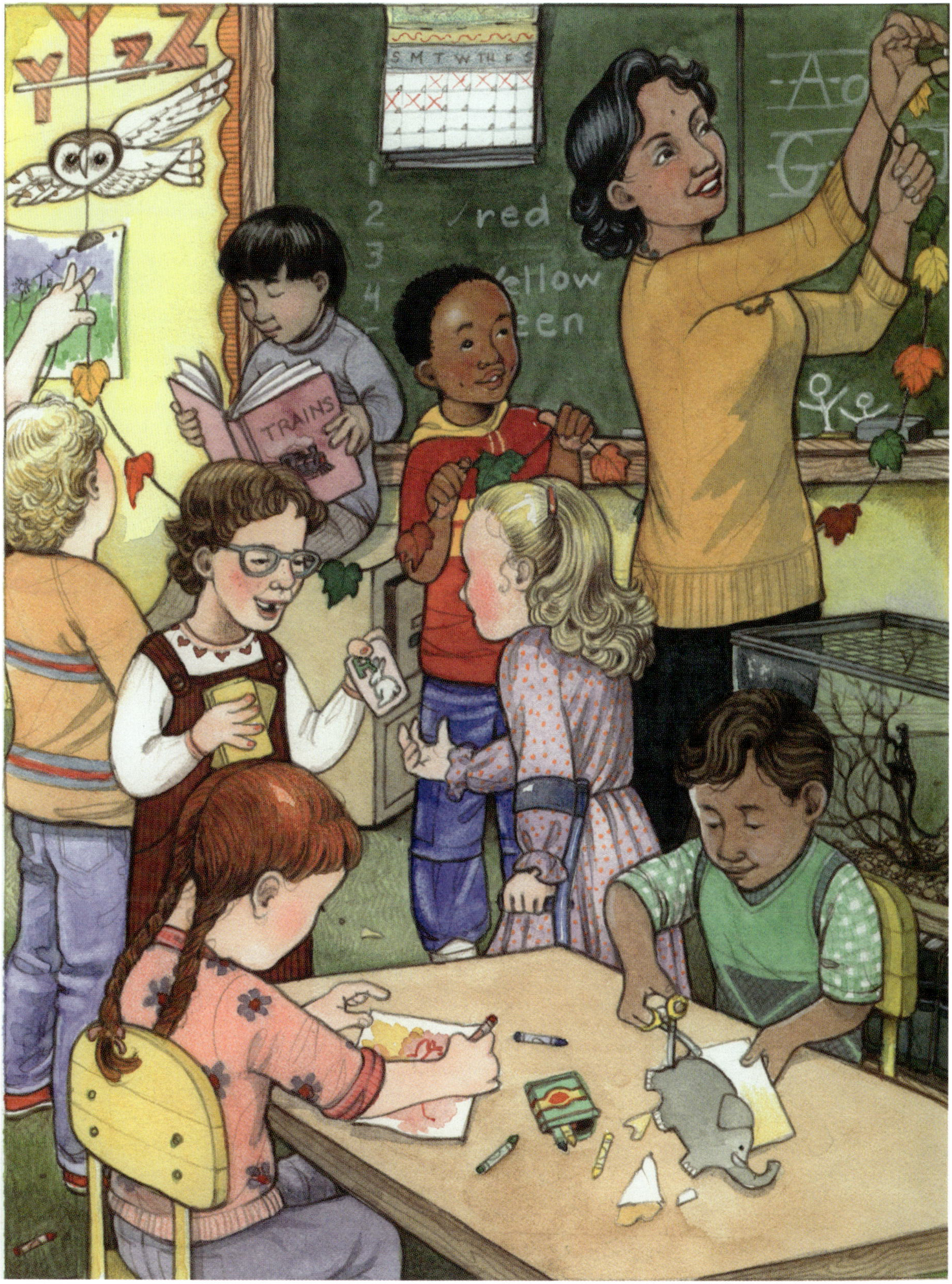
S M T W TH F S
red
TRAINS

Finally it was playground time. On the playground sat a big red, yellow, and green jungle gym next to some swings. Colby saw children already climbing up, racing to see who would reach the top first.

As Colby grabbed onto the lowest bar, he looked up. A red-haired boy with freckles was reaching the top at the same time as a dark-skinned girl with bright red barrettes in her braided hair.

"I was here first!" the boy yelled. "No black kids are allowed on this jungle gym!"

"Who says?" the girl yelled back.

"Joey and Reena!" the

teacher called out to the children. "No fighting!"

"I don't want to play with you anyway!" the girl cried out, quickly climbing down. Colby could see a tear sliding down her cheek as she ran off to join a group of black girls.

Something is really wrong here, Colby thought in alarm. At his other school, the kids all played together no matter what color their skin was or what shape their eyes were.

Mommy had always said that all the different kinds and colors of people were like a big bunch of beautiful flowers, nicest when they were all different. Colby dropped to the ground and walked slowly back to the building, thinking hard. All through the rest of school and during the bus ride home, he couldn't stop thinking about it.

Colby was really tired by the time his bus screeched to a slow stop at the corner of his street. He felt relieved when he saw Daddy waiting for him at the stop sign.

"How do you like your new school, Colby?" Daddy asked, putting his hand on Colby's shoulder.

"Fine." Colby answered quietly, staring down at the sidewalk.

"Fine?" Daddy asked. "You don't look very happy, Colby. Tell me about it."

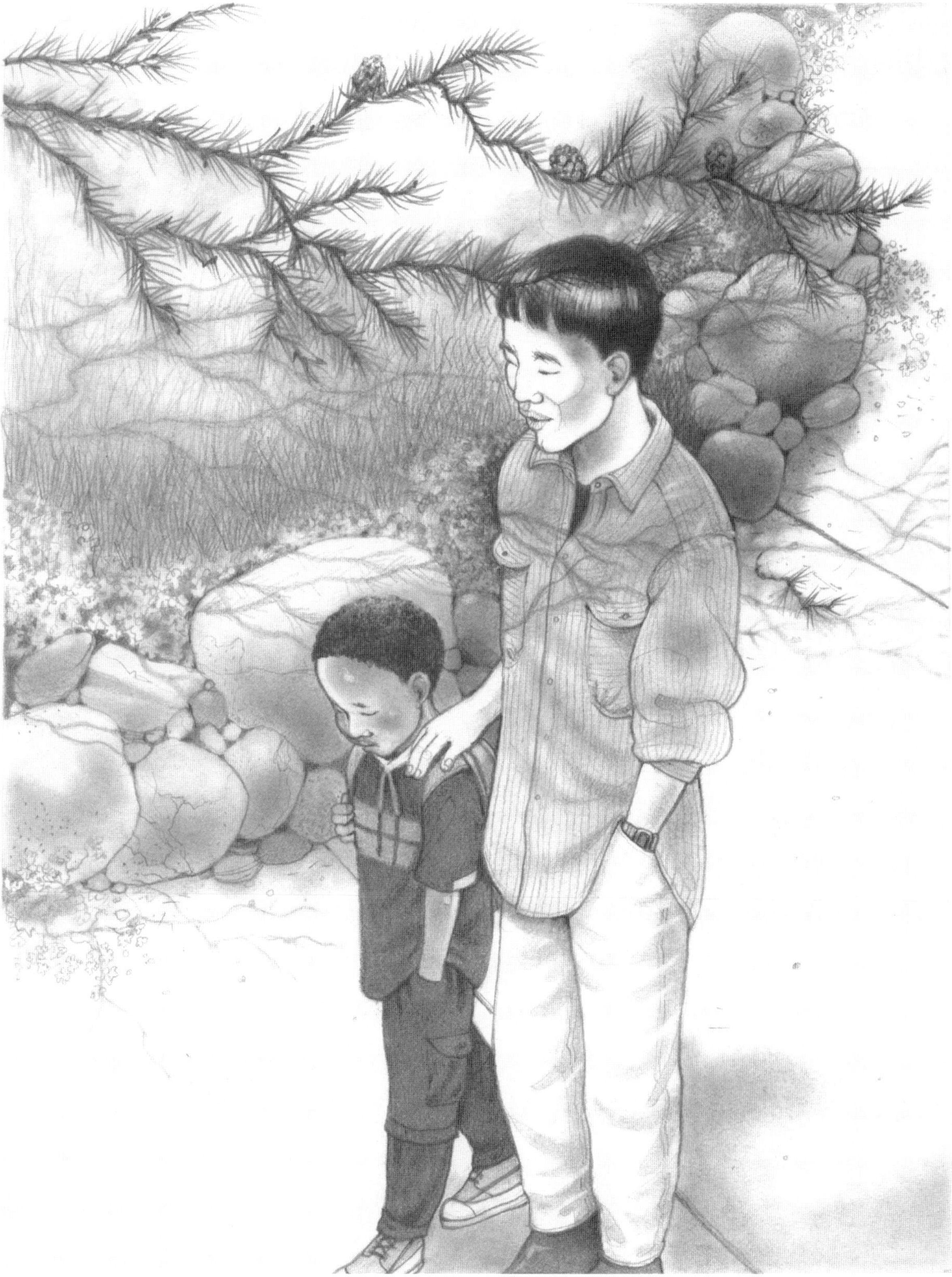

"Well, my teacher is really nice, but it seems like the kids here only like people who look like they do." Colby thought for a moment and said, "That isn't nice, is it, Daddy?" His throat tightened, and a big tear rolled down his cheek.

"No, it's not nice, Colby. It sounds as if you have some work to do to make friends with these kids."

Colby looked up at Daddy, surprised. "But how can I make friends if they don't like people who are different?"

He began to think again. *There must be a way. The kids at my other school all played together. How can I show these kids that it doesn't matter what you look like, just how nice you are?*

Colby and Daddy climbed up the big concrete steps to their new house. As Daddy opened the door, Colby saw Fluffy waiting to go out. Suddenly an idea struck him.

Maybe Fluffy can help!
She has golden fur, but other cats are different and people like them anyway. They're better all different. Maybe I can tell that to the other kids!

"Come on Fluffy!" Colby said, scooping up the soft ball of golden fur and heading back out the door.

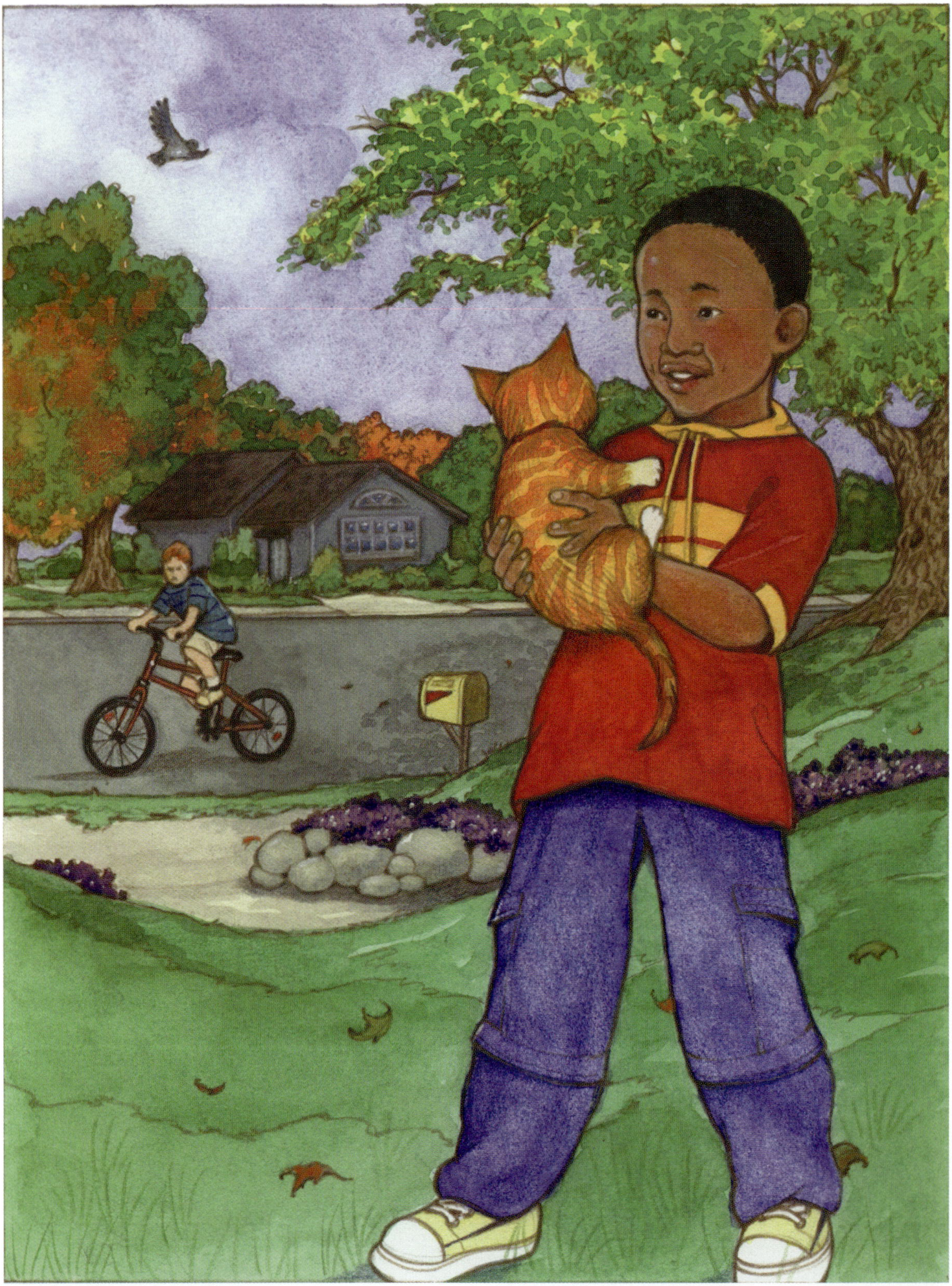

Outside, Colby looked around. He saw a kid riding down the street on a bike. It was Joey, the boy from the jungle gym! Before Colby could say anything, the boy whizzed by, making a mean face at Colby. "This could take some work." Colby said, looking down at Fluffy.

With nothing else to do, Colby put Fluffy down on the grass and started to play "pouncing tiger" with her. He was just about to make a really big pounce when he was startled by a voice behind him.

"What a cute kitten!"

Colby looked up and saw a girl holding a big calico cat. The girl's skin was very dark—almost black—and the way she talked sounded different, as if she were from another country.

"Your cat is pretty too," Colby said, picking up Fluffy so the girl could see the kitten better. "Would you like to hold her?"

"Sure!" the girl said, smiling at Colby. She put down the cat and took Fluffy gently into her arms. "I'm Elizabeth and this is my cat, Patches. Nice to meet you."

"I'm Colby and this is Fluffy," Colby smiled back as he pointed to Fluffy.

Colby squatted down to pet the other cat. "I love her different colors,"

Colby said as he began to tell her about the wonderful differences between the cats. Before he could finish, Joey came zooming up the sidewalk and across the grass ,right at them.

"Hey! Watch where you're going!" Elizabeth yelled as she and Colby and the cats jumped out of the way. Joey skidded to a stop.

"What do you have there?" he demanded. "Oh, cats. Let me see."

The girl held out Fluffy for Joey to look at. The calico rubbed herself against Colby's leg.

"Wow, one is so big and the other is so little!" Joey said in a much nicer voice.

Now is my chance, thought Colby.

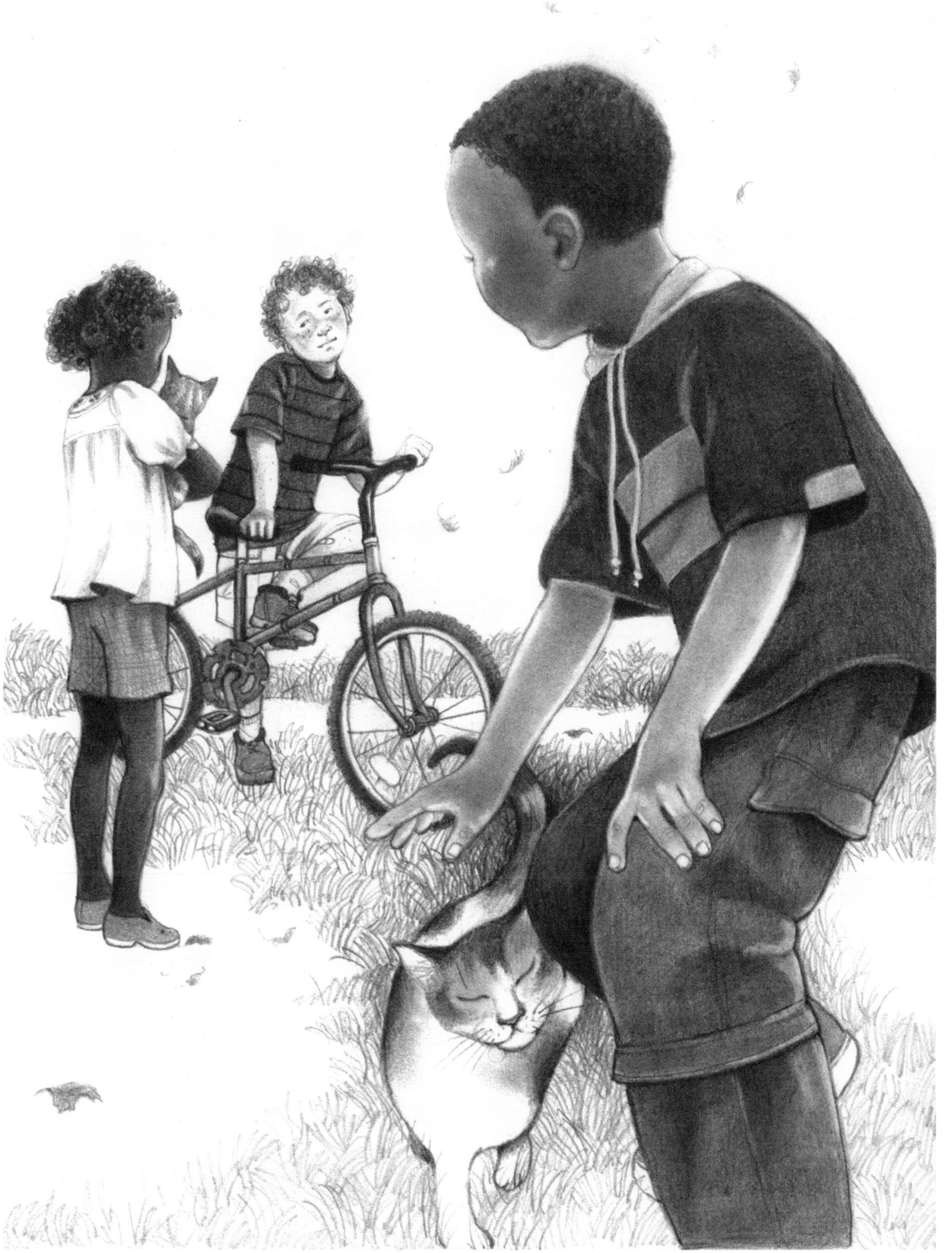

"And look at their different colors." Colby said. "One of the things that make them so interesting is that each one looks so different—just like people!" he said in a rush. Sticking his brown arm out between the freckled boy's and the girl's much darker arms, Colby said, "We're different colors too, just like the cats. And we can still be friends, even though we don't look the same."

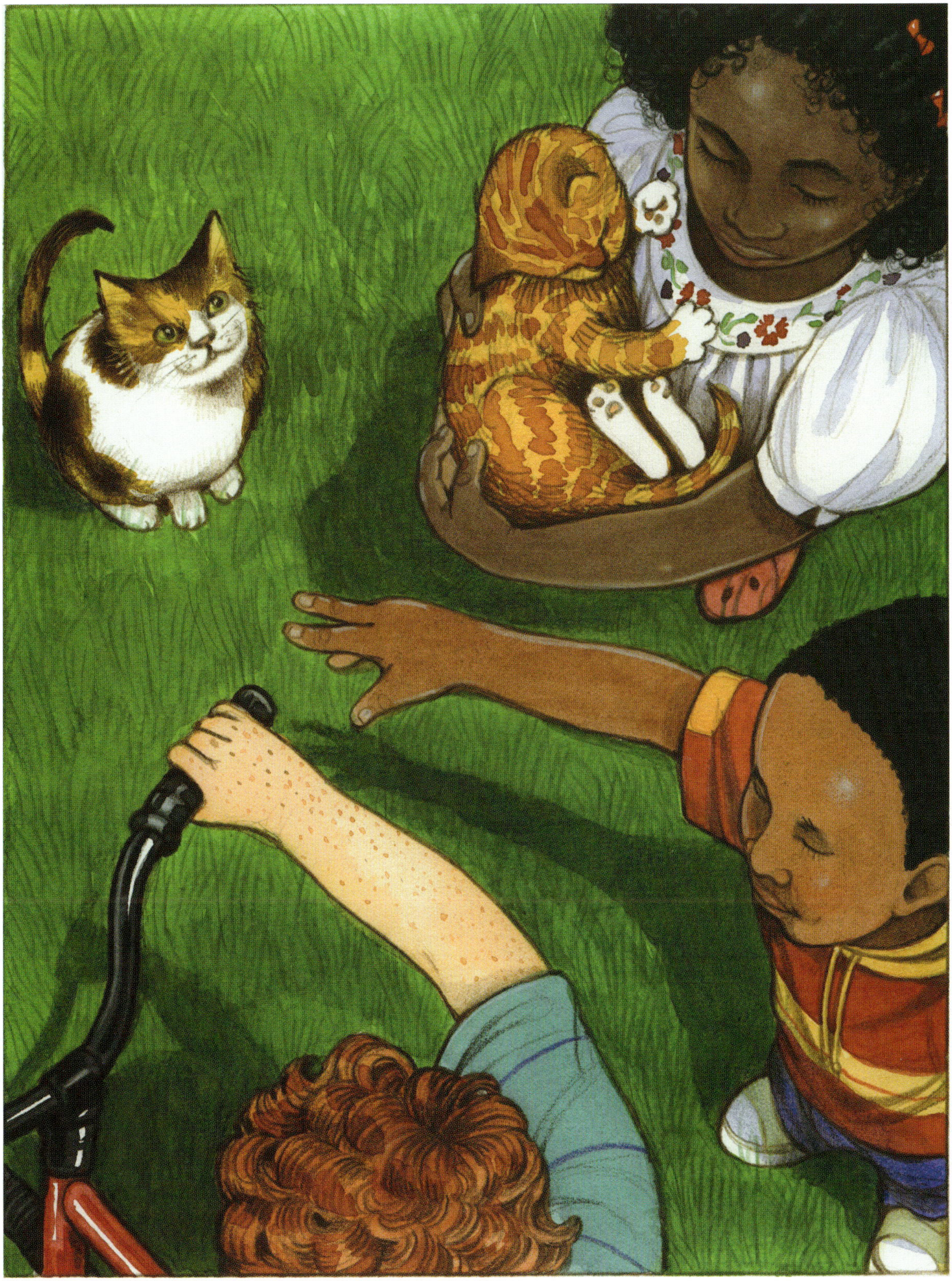

"But she talks funny too!" the boy objected, frowning.

"That's because I'm from Jamaica," said Elizabeth. "Have you always lived here?" she asked Joey, putting the squirming kitten down in the grass.

"I moved here from New York," Joey replied as he watched Fluffy stalk the bigger cat. Fluffy pounced. The cats leaped up and began to play, each pouncing and retreating. The children laughed as they watched.

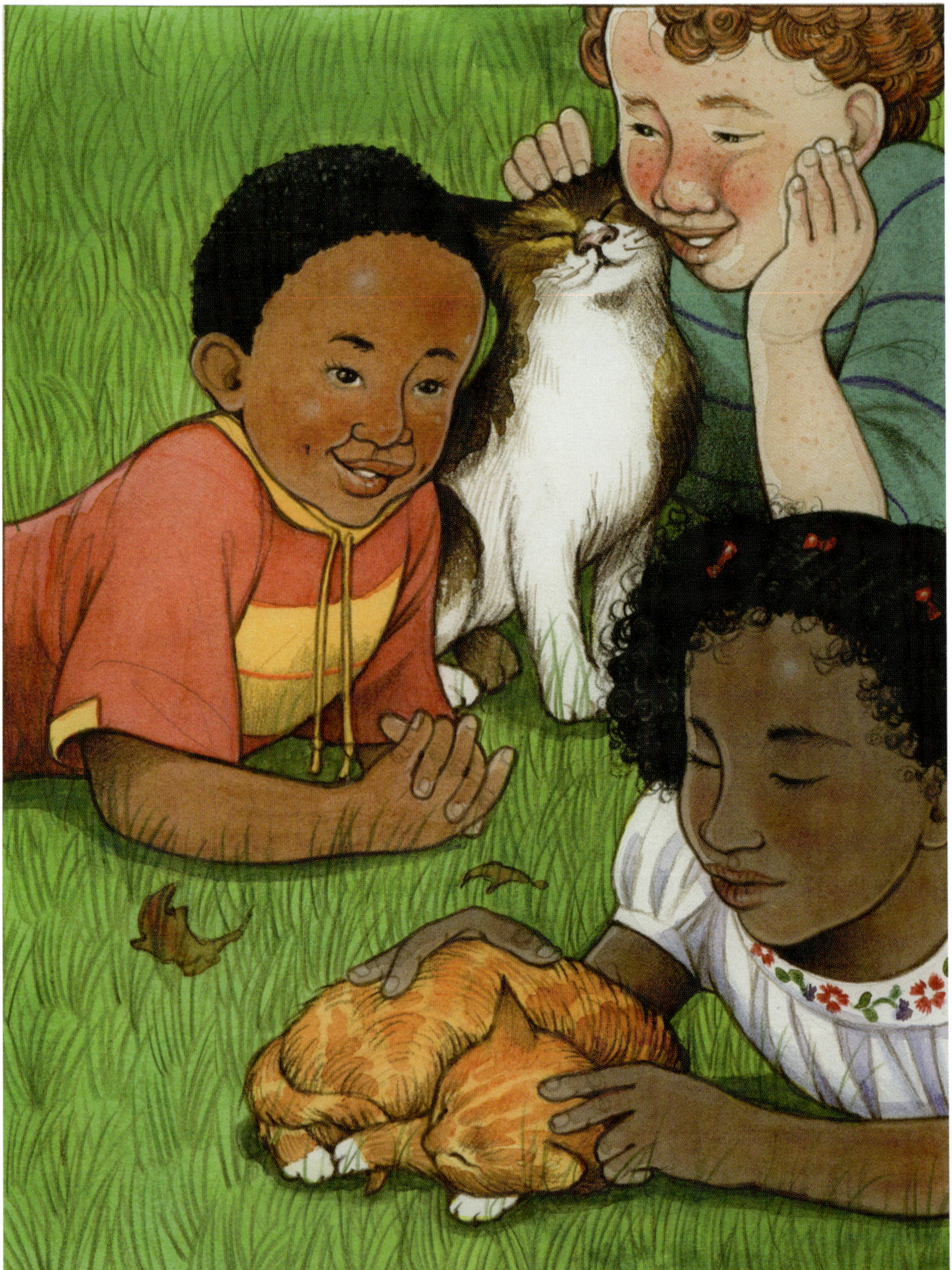

"Hey, I'm a cat!" Colby called out, crouching down to stalk the other two children. The girl and the boy crouched too, joining Colby's game of "pouncing tiger." Soon all three were rolling in the grass, laughing and playing together.

I guess it worked! Colby thought happily. *I can make friends in this new place. I could get to like it here.*

Note to Parents and Teachers: The Bahá'í Faith teaches that we must have unity among the peoples of the earth so that civilization may continue to advance. This message of unity is central to Bahá'í teachings. However, unity among the peoples of the world does not imply sameness; it implies an appreciation for the diversity of humanity through spiritual teachings. The following extracts from Bahá'í scripture provide spiritual perspective on this important theme.

"Let your vision be world-embracing, rather than confined to your own self.—*Bahá'u'lláh*

"O well-beloved ones! The tabernacle of unity hath been raised; regard ye not one another as strangers. Ye are the fruits of one tree, and the leaves of one branch.—*Bahá'u'lláh*

"Consider the flowers of a garden: though differing in kind, color and shape, yet, inasmuch as they are refreshed by the waters of one spring, revived by the breath of one wind, invigorated by the rays of one sun, this diversity increases their charm, and addeth to their beauty. Thus when that unifying force, the penetrating influence of the Word of God, taketh effect, the difference of customs, manners, habits, ideas, opinions and dispositions embellish the world of humanity. This diversity, this difference is like the naturally created dissimilarity and variety of the limbs and organs of the human body, for each one contributeth to the beauty, efficiency and perfection of the whole. When these different limbs and organs come under the influence of man's sovereign soul, and the soul's power pervadeth the limbs and members, veins and arteries of the body, then difference reinforceth harmony, diversity strengtheneth love, and multiplicity is the greatest factor for coordination."—'Abdu'l-Bahá